THE
NECROMANCER

OR,
THE TALE OF
THE BLACK FOREST

By

LAWRENCE
FLAMMENBERG

First published in 1794

British Library Cataloguing-in-Publication Data
A catalogue record for this book is available
from the British Library

Contents

LAWRENCE FLAMMENBERG

Lawrence Flammenberg was the pseudonym of German author Karl Friedrich Kahlert, born in 1765. Very little is known about his life, and he is primarily remembered for his Gothic novel, *The Necromancer; or, The Tale of the Black Forest*, first published in 1794. Consisting of a series of lurid tales of hauntings, violence and the supernatural, all set in Germany's Black Forest and featuring the resurrected wizard Volkert the Necromancer, *The Necromancer* is one of the seven 'horrid novels' lampooned by Jane Austen in *Northanger Abbey*. For a considerable amount of time, Kahlert's tale was thought not to exist except within the text of Austen's novel. Kahlert died in 1813.

THE NECROMANCER

OR,
THE TALE OF THE BLACK FOREST

When I had completed my time as a student I was appointed governor to the young Baron de R—, to conduct him on his travels. On our first journey we took our way through Italy, Switzerland, and Germany, and met, in this later place, with a most remarkable adventure.

Being arrived at the outskirts of the Black Forest, our postillion missed his way, as it began to grow dark, and at length did not know what direction he should take. Our fright was not little, when he apprised us of his distress, being desirous to get out of that dreadful forest as soon as possible, on account of the many instances of robberies and murders committed within its precincts, which the postillion had enlarged upon on the road; we therefore exhorted the fellow to go on, whatever might be the consequence. He did so, and after half an hour we came to an open spot.

'Now we are safe!' exclaimed the postillion joyfully, 'and, if I am not mistaken, not far from a village.'

He was right. We soon heard the welcome barking of dogs not far off, and a little while after we saw lights.

We entered a large village, but the inn was very different, and the landlord was amazed at the uncommon sight of gentlemen. His whole stock of eatables consisted of some smoked puddings, and a coarse sort of bread; he told us that neither wine nor beer could be got within the distance of many leagues and even our postillion could not drink his brandy. We asked him where the lord of the village resided; he answered that he never lived there, because the castle had not been habitable for many years. I enquired the reason of it.

'At present,' replied the host, 'I dare not give you an account of it, tomorrow you shall know everything; but, very likely, this night will make you guess the reason.'

The Baron and I entreated him to satisfy our curiosity, but he shook his head and left the room.

Pinched by hunger we took up with our scanty supper, and then asked the landlord to show us to our beds, but, alas! there was not one bed unoccupied in the whole house, and we were obliged to rest our weary limbs upon a bed of clean straw in the middle of the room.

The Baron soon began to snore, but I could not get a wink of sleep. Now the watchman announced the hour of midnight with a hoarse voice, and on a sudden I heard the trampling of horses and the sound of horns. The noise came nearer, and methought I heard a number of horsemen rushing by, and sounding their horns as if a large hunting party were passing through the village; the troop darted like lightning through the street close by the windows of the inn. The Baron started up, asking me with a fearful voice, 'What is this?' – 'I don't know,' replied I abruptly. I listened attentively, and the troop had not been far from our inn, when on a sudden all was again as silent as the grave; the Baron began to snore as before, and I to muse on that strange incident.

I could not think it possible that any body would go a hunting in so large a company, at that unseasonable hour, and was much inclined to think all had been a deluding dream, when I suddenly recollected the mysterious words of our landlord. I cannot but confess that I was seized with horror. I was just falling asleep when the voice of the watchman, crying one o'clock, roused me from my slumber. No sooner had he finished his round than the former noise was heard again at a small distance, I started up and ran to the window, but before I could open it the whole troop had rushed by like a hurricane. A little while after all was silent again, yet in vain did I beseech the god of slumber to take me in his arms.

The Baron had heard nothing the second time, snoring quietly by my side whilst I was ardently wishing for the morning, in order to satisfy my curiosity. I was too impatient to await the landlord's account of the castle, and when the watchman was crying two o'clock I hastened to the window, and began to converse with him.

'Watchman,' exclaimed I, 'what did that noise at twelve and one o'clock mean?' 'Your honour,' replied he, 'is certainly a stranger, for there's not a child in our village that does not know what that noise means; it is sometimes heard every night for several weeks, afterwards every thing is quiet again for a considerable time.'

'But,' said I, 'who is that person that goes a hunting at night?'

'That I can't tell you at present,' answered the watchman, 'ask your landlord, he will tell you all the particulars, I am here on my duty, and under the protection of Providence, but I dare not speak of what I hear and see.'

With these words he went away: – I wrapped myself up in my cloak, and sitting down by the window on a chair, expected, with anxious impatience, the rising of the sun. At length the eastern sky began to be embroidered with purple streaks, the crowing of the cocks sounded through the village, and the watchman announced the approach of day. The Baron awoke.

'You are very early,' said he, rubbing his eyes, 'pray tell me, what noise was it I heard in the night?'

'I myself am impatient to know it,' replied I, 'I wish the landlord would rise and unfold that mystery; the troop rushed by again at one o'clock with the same terrible noise.'

While I was talking thus, I heard the trampling of horses, and looking out of the window, saw an officer with a servant. They alighted at the inn, knocked at the door, and entered the room. The officer, a lively young man, wore a Danish uniform, and was on the recruiting business; he had missed his way like ourselves, and we soon got acquainted with him. When the Baron related the nightly adventure, the officer at first thought he was joking, but when I most seriously affirmed every circumstance, he showed an ardent desire to get acquainted with those nocturnal sportsmen.

'That honour you can easily have,' said the Baron, 'if you stay here the ensuing night, we will give you company.'

'Bravo!' exclaimed the officer, 'perhaps the gentlemen will be so polite to invite us to their sport, and then we may be so fortunate as to get a haunch of venison.'

Now the landlord entered the room. 'Well,' said he, bidding us a good morning, 'have you heard anything tonight, gentlemen?'

'More than I liked,' answered I: 'who are those sportsmen that go a hunting at midnight?'

'Why,' replied he, 'we don't talk of it: I would not tell you anything about it last night, for fear your curiosity might expose you to some misfortune; yet, having promised you yesterday to tell you as much of it as I know, I will be as good as my word.'

After having paused awhile, he began thus, in a confidential tone: 'Close by our village is a very large building, where formerly the Lord of this village used to reside. One of the former masters of the castle was a very wicked and irreligious man, who found great delight in tormenting the poor peasants; every body trembled when he appeared. He trampled with his feet upon his own children, confined them in dark dungeons, where they were often kept for many days without a morsel of bread. He used to call his tenants dogs, and to treat them as such – in short, he was cruelty itself.

'Hunting was his only amusement, and he always kept a vast number of deer, which were the ruin of the peasants' little property, and reduced them to the utmost poverty; no one dared to drive them from his fields, and if he did, he was confined in a damp dungeon, under ground, for many weeks. When that wicked man wanted to hunt, then the whole village was called together to serve him instead of dogs; if any one was not alert enough, then he would hunt him instead of the deer, till he fell down expiring under the lashes of his whip.

'One time after he had roved about from morning till night, he fell from his horse and broke his neck. He was buried in his garden. But now he was terribly punished for his wickedness, having had no rest in his grave to the present day. At certain times of the year he is doomed to appear in the village, at twelve o'clock at night, and to make his entry into the castle with his infernal crew, but as soon as the clock strikes one he is plunged back again into the lake of fire burning with brimstone. Nobody can inhabit the castle! Many who have been so fool-hardy to attempt it have lost their lives; whoever ventures to look out of the window when the infernal hosts are passing by gets a swollen face as a punishment for his curiosity. We are now used to that nocturnal sport, and do not care for those infernal spirits, but many strangers have fallen ill through fright.'

Here the landlord finished his tale, and seemed to be pleased with our astonishment; however, his pleasure was soon damped when the Lieutenant broke out in a roaring laughter.

'Laugh as long as you please,' said he; 'stay here till night if you have courage, and then we shall see if you will laugh.'

'That I will,' replied the officer, 'I will not only stay in your house, but I will also spend the coming night at that dreadful castle. I dare say, gentlemen,' added he, 'you will keep me company.'

The Baron, being a man of honour, thought it a great disgrace to betray the least want of courage in the presence of the soldier; he therefore promised to accompany him thither: I made several objections, representing to the officer the danger we should run, not knowing who those spirits might be; however, he silenced all my remonstrances: 'I am a soldier,' said he, 'and all ghosts and hobgoblins have ever been kept at a respectable distance by a martial dress.'

At length I was obliged to take a part in the expedition, if I would not desert the Baron. The landlord, who had all that time been staring at us in dumb amazement, lifted up his hands when I had consented to go to the castle, and entreated us, for God's sake, to desist from our undertaking: 'If you go,' added he, 'then all of you will be dead before tomorrow morning: for heaven's sake, dear gentlemen, do not run into the very mouth of the devil thus wantonly!'

However, the raillery of the Lieutenant put him soon so much out of temper, that he left us in great wrath, swearing in the height of his anger, that the devil would make us smart for our fool-hardiness and unbelief.

'Gentlemen,' began now the officer, 'pray let us take a walk to that terrible place, where we are going to spend the night, and reconnoitre it before dinner.' Approving of that proposal, we went all three to that residence of terror.

We approached and beheld the gothic remains of a half decayed castle, the gate was open and we entered the fabric. The arched walls, overgrown with moss and ivy, echoed to the sound of our footsteps; a long narrow passage led to a spacious courtyard, paved with stones; now we espied a spiral staircase of stone, and ascended it in dumb silence. A second long and narrow passage, which received a faint glimmering of light through several small windows, strongly guarded by iron bars, led us to a back door; the chilly damps of the long confined air rushed from the aperture when the Lieutenant had pushed it open; the apartment to which it led bore the gloomy appearance of a prison – the remains of half-decayed tapestry, covered with cobwebs, gave the room a dark dreary appearance; pieces of broken furniture were scattered about on the floor, a lamp hung in the middle from an iron chain fastened to the arched ceiling.

Just as we were going to leave this abode of gloom and horror, I perceived a little door in the remotest corner of the room, it was likewise unbolted, and we entered a second room, which bore the same gloomy aspect with the former apartment, being covered with half-rotten remains of broken furniture; another door led us at length into a spacious hall, where the cheering light of the day hailed us at last, many of the arched windows being either open or broken to pieces; the fresh air, the beautiful view meeting our eye from every side, chased at once from our countenance the solemn awe.

'Here,' exclaimed the Lieutenant, 'here we will meet the airy Lords of this Manor; Let us try, gentlemen, whether we cannot fit a table and some seats among the rotten relics of furniture.'

We succeeded in our attempt, dragged a round massy table in the middle of the hall, supported it by four worm-eaten poles, then we fetched some pieces of wood from the adjacent apartments, placing them upon large stones round the table, and thus secured a resting place for the night.

Now we rambled through several apartments on the other side of the hall, and meeting with nothing worthy of our notice, except the traces of desolation, we returned by the way we had entered that gloomy mansion.

We descended into the courtyard and made there likewise our observations: spurred on by curiosity, we entered through a ruinous side building, a garden, which still bore some marks of former grandeur; broken statues of marble were here and there lying on the ground. We cleared with our sabres a way through brambles and nettles to a grove of beech trees; it likewise was hardly penetrable.

Having worked our way for more than half an hour, with much toil and difficulty, through a thicket of thistles and brambles, we arrived at length wearied and fatigued at an open spot; in the middle of it we beheld a statue, bearing in one hand an urn of black marble – we approached and read the following inscription on the pdestal:

HIC JACET GODOFREDUS HAUSSINGERUS,
PECCATOR.
(*Here lieth Godfrey Haussinger, a Sinner.*)

A little lower down we perceived a cross engraved in the stone, and under it

A.D. 1603.

We stared at each other in dumb amazement, and being already too much fatigued, we did not like to work our way farther into the garden, and returned.

'Gentlemen,' began the officer, as we were going back, 'what do you think of the inscription on that tomb?'

'I think,' replied I, 'it strongly corroborates what the landlord had told us.'

My companion smiled, and we came again into the courtyard, looking around we observed an arched wall opposite the staircase; as we came nearer we saw a flight of steps leading to a cellar, which was shut up by a massy iron door, strongly secured by an enormous padlock.

Having now examined every corner we returned to our inn.

The landlord, who was ignorant of what we had been about, was struck with horror and amazement when we related where we had been, and did his utmost to persuade us to desist from our design; however, when he saw he was spending his breath in vain, he kept his peace, and mentioned not a single word more about it during the whole day – we did the same – for the Lieutenant's conversation amused us so well, that evening stole upon us unawares.

Our dinner was better than our scanty supper on the preceding day, because the Lieutenant had brought with him an ample provision of ham and cold beef; some bottles of excellent wine, which he was also provided with, raised our spirits, and increased his and the Baron's courage, in such a manner, that they expected the approach of night with the greatest impatience – they were constantly looking at their watches, and as soon as the clock had struck nine, thought it high time to go to the castle.

We called the landlord to pay our bill, and the poor fellow tried once more to persuade us not to go to the castle: he entreated us not to expose our lives thus daringly to certain danger, and at last fell on his knees; – but when we left the room, without taking notice of his entreaties and ardent prayers, he lamented before hand our untimely death, gave us a lamp, and bolted the door, fetching a deep sigh.

The Lieutenant's servant walked before us, carrying the lighted lamp in his hand, and a portmanteau stocked with provisions under his arm, and we kept close to his heels, armed with sabres and pistols.

It was autumn, and of course very dark. We arrived at the castle; the faint glimmering of the lamp spread a kind of awful twilight around us as we were walking through the lofty arches of the vaulted passage leading to the courtyard. Having fired our pistols and loaded them again with bullets, we ascended the staircase; the doors leading to the hall we left open, that we might have a view of the courtyard, and sat cheerfully down to supper; a bottle of wine we had taken with us to keep us alert, was handed round: however, we missed our aim, for every one of us began to grow drowsy soon after we had finished our meal – we rose and walked about in order to avoid falling asleep, but we were soon tired of it, the ground being so very uneven, and returned to our seats. I recollected now, very fortunately, that I had put the fables of Gellert in my pocket. I took the book out, and began to read to the company; then I gave it to the Baron, and he was relieved by the Lieutenant – thus we were enabled to resist the powerful charms of sleep.

Now it struck eleven. All around us was buried in awful silence, which only now and then was interrupted by the creaking of our feeble chairs; the Lieutenant wound up his watch and put it before him on the table.

'One hour more,' began now the officer, 'and we shall be in another world.' Then he awoke his servant, who was fast asleep, and the Baron began again to read to us. – When the Lieutenant's turn came for the second time, he looked at his watch and exclaimed, 'three quarters past eleven, we must be on our guard.'

He got up and went to the window, I followed him, impenetrable darkness surrounded us, no star could be seen; awful silence was still all around, interrupted only by the snoring John, and the creaking of the wood; the pale light of our lamp produced a horrid glimmering in the spacious dreary hall; the Baron, leaning his head upon his arm, struggled to forget every object around him, and the officer uttered not a single word.

Now we heard a clock toll twelve at a great distance, and I walked softly back to my seat, the Lieutenant did the same, taking up one of his pistols, and rubbing the lock with his handkerchief. We looked at each other, and every one of us strove in vain to hide the horror he was struggling against. The watchman cried the hour, the crowing of the cocks told us midnight was set in, and still all round us was as silent as the grave. The Baron laid the book upon the table, and the Lieutenant was going to raise a loud laughter, asking us where the spirits might be, when suddenly the trampling of horses and the sound of horns was heard – we all were fixed to our seats, staring at each other with a ghastly look; now the noise seemed to be under our window; the Lieutenant ran towards it, with a cocked pistol in his hand, but he was too late.

All was quiet again, and an awful stillness swayed around the castle: however, a few seconds after we heard suddenly a most tremendous noise in the courtyard, which was followed by a terrible trampling and a jingling of spurs on the staircase, as if a great number of people in boots was coming up. The noise came nearer and nearer, my feet began to fail, my teeth to chatter in my mouth, and my hair to rise like bristles, while every sense was lost in anxious bodings; at length the noise grew fainter and fainter, and soon we could hear it no more, and midnight stillness resumed her awful sway.

A long pause of dumb astonishment ensued, until at last the Lieutenant, who had recovered his spirits first, exclaimed, 'Shall we go down?' I shook my head without uttering a word, and the Baron was likewise silent. 'Then I will go alone,' said the Lieutenant, snatched up a brace of pistols, drew his sabre, and hurried down. He returned a few minutes after, exclaiming, 'It is surprising; I cannot see the least traces of either men or horses.'

Now he retook his seat, casting down his looks in a pensive

manner – his servant was still snoring – the Baron began again to read, and I fell fast asleep. At once I was roused by the report of a pistol, I and honest John started up at the same moment, and we heard once more the trampling of horses and the sound of horns, but it soon died away at a distance, and the Lieutenant entered the hall with the Baron.

They also had not been able to resist the leaden wand of sleep, but the same noise in the courtyard we had heard at twelve o'clock had soon roused them from their slumber. 'As soon as we heard the noise,' said the Baron, 'we hastened to the outer room, our pistols cocked, but before we could reach it the noise was under the window of the castle; the Lieutenant knocked through one of the windows in the room close to the hall, and sent a bullet after the troop, which was rushing by like a hurricane; however, he was prevented by the darkness of the night from distinguishing anything except some white horses.

'The spirits are afraid of us,' exclaimed the Lieutenant now, 'but come, let us return to our inn, we shall rest more comfortable on a bed of clean straw than on this damp ground.' We all consented to it, and left the gloomy abode of those nocturnal sportsmen. We knocked a good while at the door of the inn before it was opened: and at last the landlord appeared, stammering, lost in wonder, 'God be praised that you are still alive, how did you escape?'

The Lieutenant silenced him by some hasty lies, and promised to give him a full account of the whole adventure after he should have rested a little.

'Gentlemen,' said he, as soon as he got up in the morning, 'next night I will go once more to the haunted castle, and spend the night in the courtyard, will you keep me company?'

The Baron looked at me if he wished me to refuse the proposal; I did so. 'We cannot,' said I, 'stay here a day longer, and such an undertaking would, besides, be too dangerous for only four people.'

'Oh!' exclaimed the Lieutenant, 'if that is all you have to say against it, then I will soon make you easy. We will take a dozen stout fellows from the village with us, they will not hesitate to accompany us if we give them a couple of dollars and a good dram; it will be devilish good fun, and tomorrow, with the first dawn of day, I will depart with you.'

The Baron consented to the proposal, and I myself did not dislike it; in short, we remained, and sent out postillion through the village to publish, 'that all young fellows who would go with us to the castle next night, should have sixpence each, and as much brandy as they could drink.'

In less than half an hour the whole village was assembled round the door of the inn. We selected fifteen of the stoutest, ordered them to provide themselves with proper arms, and to appear by ten o'clock at night at the inn. Our landlord, who beheld these preparations in dumb amazement, believed firmly that we must be arch necromancers, and his fancy having been fired by the wonderful account of our nocturnal adventure, which the Lieutenant had given him, he was himself not unwilling to go with us to the castle, and to bid defiance to the infernal hosts. However, as soon as it grew dark, his courage died away, and he wished success to our undertaking, telling us, he could not leave his house.

Our little army was assembled before ten o'clock, armed with scythes, poles, hay forks, and flails. We ordered the landlord to give a dram to every one: took some tables, benches, lamps, and a small cask of brandy with us, and marched in triumph towards the castle.

We pitched our camp in the courtyard, not far from the entrance, the peasants placed themselves round the brandy cask, lighted their pipes, and expected with pleasure the appearance of the airy gentlemen.

Another advantage we reaped from that honest company was, that we had no need to keep sleep at a distance by reading, for the merriment of our little army soon rose to the highest pitch, and these jovial fellows, being heated by the contents of our little cask, challenged his satanic majesty and all his infernal hosts amid peals of roaring laughter.

It was now past eleven o'clock, and the nose began to abate, some of our gentlemen were nodding, and some snoring, we were therefore obliged to beg those who had not yielded to the powerful charms of sleep, to give us a song, which they instantly did in so vociferous a manner, that our hearing organs were most painfully affected – the sleepers started up when they heard that terrible noise, and joined the jovial songsters with all their might. Thus we chased away the god of sleep, who seemed not in the least to relish the disharmonious notes of our jolly companions.

Now the Lieutenant beckoned to the blithesome crew, and the clamorous noise was suddenly hushed in awful silence. It struck twelve o'clock, and the sound of horns and the trampling of horses was heard at a distance. The peasants listened, their mouths wide open, and gazed at each other struck with chilly terror. No sound was heard, except the palpitating of their hearts, and here and there the chattering of teeth – all of them moved their lips as if praying ardently. The noise came nearer and nearer, and now it seemed to be in the castle. Again everything was silent, but in an instant the former noise struck once more our listening ears, and the infernal hosts rushed by like lightning – the Lieutenant, the Baron, and I darted through the passage leading to the gate, but the airy gentlemen were already out of sight, and we could see nothing, save a faint glimmering of some white horses. The mingled noise of their horns and of the trampling of their horses soon died away; the stillness of midnight swayed all around, and we returned to the courtyard.

Our valiant crew was still fixed to the ground, seized with horror and astonishment. None of them were able to distinguish whether we were ghosts or their fellow-adventurers; however, they recovered their spirits by degrees, and prepared to leave the residence of the infernal sportsmen.

We left the castle, fully convinced that these nocturnal ramblers must be being who were afraid of us, discharged our courageous troop and went to rest.

I awoke with the first ray of the morning sun, and roused the Baron and the Lieutenant; the latter seemed not to be inclined to fulfil his promise, being desirous to try his fortune once more, and to hide himself either in the courtyard, or before the gate. When he saw that we would stay not any longer, he postponed the execution of his design to a future time, and followed our example.

We left our inn at six o'clock, the morning was gloomy and rainy, the wind swept furiously over the heath, and drove the black clouds still closer and closer together; after a few minutes we entered the Black Forest. Looking out of the coach I saw the Lieutenant and his servant turn to the left towards a brook, where we beheld an odd incident. A reverend old man was sitting there, and reading in a large book; bewildered in profound meditation, he seemed to take no notice of the howling storm; and not to be sensible of the rain rushing down in large drops upon his uncovered head, the tempest was sporting with his reverend grey locks, and the rain beating in his face, yet he did not stir. His long brown robe seemed to denote a traveller from the East – a long staff and a black wallet were lying by his side.

I got out of the coach to view that strange being a little closer, and to speak to him, but before I could accost him, the Lieutenant exclaimed, 'Greybeard, what art thou reading?'

The old man appeared to take no notice of his question, and went on reading as if nobody had been there.

'What art thou reading?' exclaimed the Lieutenant once more, alighting and looking over his shoulder at the book.

The old man answered not a word, but still continued to read. I also was now standing behind him, and looking at the book, its leaves were of yellow parchment, the characters large and of different colours.

The Baron was close at my heels, and the Lieutenant being provoked by the man's obstinate silence, shook him now violently by the shoulder, thundering in his ears, 'Greybeard, what art thou reading?'

Now the old man lifted his reverend head slowly up, stared at us with angry looks, and then said, with a solemn awful voice,
'Wisdom!'
'What language is it?'
OLD MAN – (Reading again) – 'The language of wisdom.'
'What dost thou call wisdom?'
OLD MAN – 'All that thou dost not comprehend.'
LIUETENANT – 'If thou knowest what other people cannot comprehend, then I should like to ask thee a question.'
OLD MAN – (Staring again at him) – 'What question?'
LIEUTENANT – 'There is a castle not far from the next village, where every night a numerous troop of spirits make their entry; I and these two gentlemen have watched there these two nights.'
OLD MAN – (Interrupting him) – 'And art not a bit wiser for't, for thou seemest not to be fit to converse with spirits.'
LIEUTENANT – 'But thou – ?'
OLD MAN – 'I understand the language of Wisdom.'
The Lieutenant bit his lips, shaking his head with a contemptuous smile. Now the Baron accosted the old man, who again was immersed in profound meditation.
BARON – 'Well, then, if thy book contains such a treasure of wisdom, then tell us why that castle is haunted by spirits, and for what reason they go their nightly rounds?'
OLD MAN – 'That the spirits must tell thee themselves.'
BARON – 'What does then thy book contain?'
OLD MAN – 'The ways and means of forcing them to a confession.'
BARON – 'But why hast thou not forced them long ago to confess every thing?'
OLD MAN – 'Because I never cared for it.'
BARON – (Laughing) – 'But if we should entreat thee to do it, and pull our purses, would'st thou not do us that favour?'
OLD MAN – (Frowning) – 'Vile mortal, can wisdom be bought with gold and silver?'

BARON – 'How can one then purchase it?'

OLD MAN – 'With nothing – hast thou courage?'

BARON – 'Else we could not have watched in the dreadful castle.'

OLD MAN – 'Then spend another night in it. I will be there a quarter before twelve o'clock – now leave me.'

We gazed at each other with doubtful looks. The old man resumed his reading, and seemed to take no further notice of us, who were still standing behind him lost in silent wonder. At length the Lieutenant mounted his horse, and we went back to our coach. 'Well,' said the officer, as we were getting in our carriage, 'well, gentlemen, will you return with me?'

In vain did I make objections, the expectation of the two hot-headed young men was strained too much; it was impossible to subdue the eager curiosity of the young Baron, and the presence of the Lieutenant made me apprehend that all reasoning would not only be spent in vain, but at the same time make me contemptible; I therefore was forced to go back with them, and to embark in an enterprise, which, being not only useless, but also very dangerous, would plunge me in great distress.

Our host was highly rejoiced and struck with astonishment, when he saw us come back with the intention (as he believed) to engage once more with the nightly sportsmen. Our valiant companions of the preceding night had given a wonderful account of our adventure, relating how horribly the ghosts had looked, how courageously they had encountered the infernal crew, and how the strange conjurors at last had banished the tremendous host from the castle for ever.

The whole village assembled, therefore, as soon as our return was known, gazing at us as supernatural beings, and consulting us about several matters. The Lieutenant had his fun with the simplicity of those honest people and the day was spent merrily.

It was already dark, and the villagers had not yet left the inn; they unanimously entreated us to take them along with us to the castle. We were obliged to disavow our design, to feign sleepiness, and to order a bed of straw to be got ready.

At ten o'clock we stole silently to the castle without a light; the Lieutenant's servant lighted our lamp in the courtyard, and we went to the hall, where we had spent the first night, waiting with impatience for the last quarter before midnight. The Lieutenant did not believe the old man would be as good and his word; I joyfully seconded his opinion, and should have been glad if we had not waited for him; but the Baron, who, from his juvenile days, had been fond of every thing bearing the aspect of mysteriousness, was quite charmed with the reverend appearance of the old man, and maintained, upon his honour, that he certainly would stick to his appointment.

The Lieutenant began to discourse with the Baron on apparitions and necromancers, maintaining by experience and reasoning, that all was either deceit or the effects of a deluded fancy; yet the Baron would not relinquish his opinion, adding, that one ought not to speak lightly of those matters, and that the old man certainly would prove the truth of his assertion. We were still conjecturing who that strange wanderer might be, when we saw by our watches that there were but sixteen minutes wanting to twelve; as soon as it was three quarters after eleven we heard the sound of gentle steps in the passage.

'Our greybeard,' said the Lieutenant, 'is a man of honour,' and took up the lamp to meet the old man.

Now he entered the hall, his black wallet on his back, and beckoned in a solemn manner to follow him. We did so, and he led us through the apartments and the vaulted passage down stairs. We followed him through the courtyard to the iron gate of the cellar without uttering a word; there he stopped, turning towards us, and eyeing us awhile with a ghastly look; after an awful pause of expectation, he said with a low trembling voice, 'Don't utter a word as you value your lives.' Then he went down the two first steps; taking from his bosom an enormous key which had been suspended round his neck by an iron chain, and opened, without the least difficulty, the monstrous padlock, the door flew open, and the old man took the lamp from the Lieutenant, leading us down a large staircase of stone; we descended into a spacious cellar, vaulted with hewn stone, and beheld all around large iron doors, secured by strong padlocks; our hoary leader went slowly towards an iron folding door, opposite to the staircase, and opened it likewise with his key; it flew suddenly open, and we beheld with horror a black vault, which received a faint light from a lamp suspended to the ceiling by an old chain.

The old man entered, uncovered his reverend head, and we did the same, standing by his side in trembling expectation, awed by the solemnity that reigned around us; a dreaful chilliness seized us, we felt the grasp of the icy fangs of horror, being in a burying vault surrounded by rotten coffins. Skulls and mouldered bones rattled beneath our feet, the grisly phantom of death stared in our faces from every side, with a grim, ghastly aspect. In the centre of the vault we beheld a black marble coffin, supported by a pedestal of stone, over it was suspended to the ceiling a lamp spreading a dismal, dying glimmering around. The air was heavy and of a musty smell, we could hardly respire, the objects around seemed to be wrapped in a blue mist. The hollow sound of our footsteps reechoed through the dreary abode of horror as we walked closer.

The old man stopped at a small distance from the marble coffin, beckoning to us to come closer; we moved slowly on, and he made a sign not to advance farther than he could reach with extended arms. The Lieutenant placed himself at his right, I took my station at his left, and the Baron opposite to him.

He put the lamp on the ground before him, taking his book, an ebony wand, and a box of white plate out of his wallet. Out of the latter he strewed a reddish sand around him, drew a circle with his wand, and folded his hands across the breast, then he pronounced, amid terrible convulsions, some mysterious words, opened the book and began to read, whilst his face was distorted in a ghastly manner; his convulsions grew more horrible as he went on reading; all his limbs seemed to be contracted by a convulsive fit. His eyebrows shrunk up, his forehead was covered with wrinkles, and large drops of sweat were running down his cheeks – at once he threw down his book, gazing with a strange look, and his hands lifted up at the marble coffin.

We soon perceived that midnight had set in; the trampling of horses and the sound of horns was heard, the Necromancer did not move a limb, still staring at the coffin with a haggard look. Now the noise was on the staircase of the cellar and still he was motionless, his eyes being unmovingly directed towards the coffin. But now the noise was in the cellar, he brandished his wand and all around was buried in awful silence. He pronounced again three times an unintelligible word with a horrible thundering voice. A flash of lightning hissed suddenly through the dreary vault, lighting the damp walls, and a hollow clap of thunder roared through the subterraneous abode of chilly horror. The light in the lamp was now extinguished, silence and darkness swayed all around; soon after we heard a gentle rustling just before us, and a faint glimmer was spreading through the gloomy vault. It grew lighter and lighter, and we soon perceived rays of dazzling light shooting from the marble coffin, the lid of which began to rise higher and higher; at once the whole vault was illuminated, and a grisly human figure rose slow and awful from the coffin. The phantom, which was wrapped up in a shroud, bore a dying aspect, it trembled violently as it rose and emitted a hollow groan, looking around with chilly horror. Now the spectre descended from the pedestal, and moved with trembling steps and haggard looks towards the circle where we were standing.

'Who dares,' groaned it, in a faltering hollow accent; 'who dares to disturb the rest of the dead?'

'And who art thou?' replied our leader, with a threatening frowning aspect, 'who art thou, that thou darest to disturb the stillness of this castle, and the nocturnal slumber of those that inhabit its environs?'

The phantom shuddered back, groaning in a most lamentable

accent, 'Not I, not I, my cursed husband disturbs the peace around and mine.'

OLD MAN – 'For what reason?'

GHOST – 'I was assassinated, and he who judges men has thrown my sins upon the murderer.'

OLD MAN – 'I comprehend thee, unhappy spirit, betake thyself again to rest; by my power, which every spirit dreads, he shall disturb thee no more – begone –'

The phantom bowed respectfully, staggered towards the pedestal, climbed up, got into the coffin, and disappeared; the lid sunk slowly down, and the light which had illuminated the dismal mansion of mortality died away by degrees. A flash of lightning hissed again through the vault, licking the damp walls, the hollow sound of thunder roared through the subterraneous abode of horror, the lamp began to again burn, and the awful silence of the grave swayed all around.

The old man took up his wallet and his book, beckoning us to follow him. We returned to the adjoining vault, through which we had entered that abode of awful dread; it was as lonesome as we had left it; our leader locked the iron folding-door carefully; then he took out his wallet a large piece of parchment on which a number of strange characters were written, a piece of black sealing wax, and a monstrous iron seal. Having made several crosses over these things with his ebony wand, he fixed the parchment above the lock, and sealed it hastily on the four corners.

This done, he went into the middle of the cellar assigning us our places; then he strewed sand on the ground, drew a circle with his wand, and began again to read in his book amid horrible convulsions. He brandished his wand, pronouncing three times with a most tremendous voice the same word he had made use of in the burying vault. A flash of lightning hissed through the cellar, a clap of thunder shook the subterraneous fabric, all the doors save that which had been sealed up were suddenly forced open with a thundering noise, the lamp was extinguished, and a blue light reflected in a grisly manner from the stairacse against the damp wall; woeful groans, lamentations, and the dismal clashing of chains resounded through the spacious caverns. The noise seemed to come from the staircase – gentle steps were heard – a numerous troop seemed to be descending into the cellar; the lamentations and the woeful groans advanced nearer, and louder resounded the clashing of chains.

Horrid to behold, did now a second phantom appear before our gazing looks, staggering slowly towards us, and leaving a numerous retinue on the staircase; the garment of the spectre was stained with blood, the skull fractured, the eyes like two portentous comets!

'Who art thou?' roared our leader with a thundering voice, and the dreary cavern echoed to the sound.

The phantom answered with a hollow, dismal voice, 'A damned soul!'

OLD MAN – 'What business hast thou in this castle?'

GHOST – 'I want to be redeemed from hell.'

OLD MAN – 'How canst thou be redeemed?'

GHOST – 'By the forgiveness of my wife.'

OLD MAN – 'How darest thou claim it, reprobate villain?
 Return to thy damned companions in hell. Respect this seal,
 respect these characters.'

Here the old man pointed at the door of the vault which had been sealed up: the phantom staggered towards it, but suddenly shuddered back and sunk groaning on the ground; a flash of lightning illuminated the cellar, and a tremendous peal of thunder resounded through the lofty vault; all the doors were shut again with a terrible noise, a frightful howling filled our ears, and horrid phantoms hovered before our eyes; flashes of lightning hissed through the vault and roaring claps of thunder threatened to overturn the whole fabric.

The lightning ceased by degrees, and the roaring of the thunder died away, a blue flame was still glimmering on the staircase, but it soon died away, and we were surrounded with darkness; groans and dreadful lamentations resounded still through the winding caverns, but soon all around was hushed in profound silence. After a short pause of horrid stillness, the trampling of horses and the sound of horns was heard again; yet that noise died away also before we recovered our recollection.

When our astonishment began to subside, we perceived that we were standing in a dark cellar, without knowing whether any one of us was missing. A disagreeable sulphurous odour affected our smelling organs, and bereft us almost of the power of respiration; not a whisper interrupted the dead midnight silence which surrounded us. At length, somebody took me by the hand, I shuddered back, my imagination being still the wrestling place of horrid wild phantoms, and my soul divining a thousand dreadful thoughts.

'It is I,' said the Lieutenant, and I felt at once as if a heavy load had been taken from my breast. Now the Baron also began to speak, 'Where are you?' whispered he, 'are you still alive?'

We groped about in the dark, and at last found him leaning against the wall.

'How shall we get out of this cursed residence of horror?' exclaimed the Lieutenant. 'Come, let us try whether we can find the staircase. It must be just opposite to us, if I am not mistaken.' Then he began to walk on, and we groped after him, tumbling now and then over loose stones.

'I have found the staircase,' cried our fellow adventurer, 'at last, after a long fruitless search, I feel the first step.'

A ray of joy beamed through our hearts as we were climbing up, but alas! it was soon most cruelly damped; the cellar door was locked up, and the blood congealed in our veins when the Lieutenant told it us. We exerted all our strength to force it open, but in vain, it was bolted on the outside. The Lieutenant called as loud as he could for his servant, whom he had left snoring in the hall; we joined our voices with his, calling with all our might, 'John! John!'

The hollow echo repeated in a tremendous accent, John! John! but no human footstep would gladden our desponding hearts.

Frantic with black despair did we now begin to knock at the massy door till the blood was running down from our hands, and to cry John, John, till our voices grew hoarse – the hollow echo still repeated in an awful tremendous accent our knocking and crying, but no human footstep was heard. 'The fellow sleeps and cannot hear us,' said the Lieutenant, at length with a faint voice, 'let us sit down and watch him when he shall come down.'

We did so, but I had no hope that the servant would come, yet I concealed my apprehension within my breast. The Lieutenant dissembled to be easy, and began to converse on what we had seen and heard; however his broken accent, the faltering of his speech, and his low voice, betrayed the anxiety of his mind. The Baron and I spoke little, and when we had been sitting about an hour not one uttered a word more; all was silent around us. Nothing interrupted the death-like stillness of the night, except the violent beating of our hearts.

At length the Lieutenant asked if we were asleep; however, the anxiety of our minds and the dreadful apprehensions which assailed us, drove far away even the idea of sleep. We sat some hours in the dreadful situation, and it was now about five o'clock in the morning when the Lieutenant exclaimed, 'I fear we wait in vain for my servant, he cannot sleep so fast that he should not hear us! But where can he be?' Then he began again to knock violently against the massy iron door, but all was in vain. No human footsteps were heard, we remained some hours on the staircase, but all our waiting and listening was fruitless, no cheering sound of human footsteps would gladden our desponding hearts.

'I will not torment you by vain apprehensions,' began the Lieutenant at length, 'however, we seem to be doomed to destruction, yet let us try if we cannot escape some way or other, come down with me into the cellar, there we shall have a better chance to espy an outlet than here.'

We descended, with trembling knees, without saying a word, and groped along in the dark a good while, knocking our heads against the damp wall, and the iron doors. Alas! our search seemed to be in vain, and the grim spectre of a lingering death stared us grisly in the face, my feet could support me no longer, and I dropped down wearied with anxiety.

Now I began to reproach myself for having plunged into the gulph of destruction not only myself but also him who had been entrusted to my care. The apprehension of being famished in that infernal abode, thrilled my soul with horror and black despair; at first I heard the Baron and the Lieutenant still groping about; neither of them uttered a word; the hollow sound of their footsteps re-echoed horribly through the vault – at length the sound of the Baron's footsteps died away at a distance, and only one of my companions in destruction remained with me.

'Where are you?' exclaimed the Lieutenant.

'Here I am,' replied I, 'but where is the Baron?'

The Lieutenant called him, and I did the same, but we received no answer. At once a sudden hollow noise struck our ears, and at the same time a faint glimmering of light darted from a remote corner of our dungeon. I started up, half frantic with joy, and we pursued the gladdening ray of light; it seemed to come from an opening in the wall. No words can express the rapture we felt when we beheld one of the iron doors half open; we went through it with hasty steps, and entered a long vaulted passage. A faint dawn of light hailed our joyful looks at a great distance from below. We descended a declivity, the farther we went the more the light increased, at length we reached the end of the avenue, and perceived some steps leading into a spacious apartment, at the entrance of which some boards on the floor had given way. We descended the steps, and, who can paint the horror which rushed upon us, when we beheld the Baron lying lifeless in the deep vault, upon some mouldering straw? I leaped down without a moment's hesitation, the Lieutenant did the same, and now we began to shake the Baron till we at length perceived signs of returning life. We continued our endeavours to recall his senses, he breathed, gave a hollow groan, and opened his eyes: his fainting fit had been the effect of sudden terror, and he had not received the least hurt.

He now told us that he had met in the dark with a long narrow passage which he had pursued, in a kind of insensibility, till he had staggered down from an elevated spot, when the boards suddenly gave way, dragging him along into the deep vault.

Looking around we perceived that we were in a spacious cavern, which appeared to have been formerly a kind of stable. High over our heads were two large round holes, grated with strong iron bars, through which the daylight was admitted, and after a closer examination we espied a gloomy outlet in a remote corner, shut up by a wooden door, which we forced open without difficulty. We now ascended through a dark passage, higher and higher, till we at length with rapture beheld an outlet which opened into the garden; we were obliged to cut our way with our sabres, through the underwood and the entangled weeds, and soon came to the courtyard. Tears of joy sparkled in our eyes, rays of unspeakable rapture beamed through our hearts, and we praised God for our unexpected deliverance from the grisly jaws of a lingering death.

The dreary desolated courtyard appeared to us a paradise, the dazzling splendour of the bright morning sun, and the pure air which we now inhaled, filled our hearts with the strongest sensations of bliss. We congratulated each other on our resurrection from the dreary abode of mortality, where we were doomed to be entombed alive, and shook each other by the hand half frantic with joy.

We went now to the hall in search of the Lieutenant's servant; the table and everything was in the same condition we had left them, but John was not there. We went through the whole gloomy fabric shouting and hallooing, discharging our pistols, but no sound was heard except the hollow echo repeating our shouts and the reports of our pistols all over the dreary building.

'Very likely he is returned to the inn,' said the Lieutenant, 'and we shall find him there.'

We left that dangerous abode of black horror, praising God

again and again for our deliverance.

As we entered the inn we beheld the landlord surrounded by a number of villagers, who were come to enquire whether we were returned from the castle. They were very much surprised when we entered the room, and, respectfully taking off their hats, told us, that the uproar at the village last night had been more tremendous than ever. Every one was impatient to know the particulars of our adventure, but the Lieutenant having then no inclination of amusing himself with their simplicity, gave them a short answer, and asked the landlord where his servant was.

'I have not seen him since yesterday,' replied he.

'It is impossible,' resumed the Lieutenant; 'where are the horses?'

'They are in the stable,' replied the landlord, 'I have just been looking after them.'

The Lieutenant gave us an apprehensive look, and begged the gaping peasants to look after him, all over the village and the adjacent places: they all were very willing to do it, and left the inn.

It was nine o'clock when we entered the inn, and it struck twelve when our honest villagers returned, with the disagreeable news that they could find poor John nowhere.

The Lieutenant thought it not prudent to remain any longer at that fatal place; the Baron likewise wished to depart and I too was impatient to be gone. As soon as we had finished our scanty dinner, we departed a second time; the tears started from the landlord's eyes, and from those of the good villagers, when we bade them farewell, after having made them a small present, and they saw us depart with regret.

The Lieutenant knew the ways through the Black Forest pretty well, he rode by our chaise leading his servant's horse with one hand, and we reached without any further accident the limits of that dreadful forest. We parted company at the close of the second day, bidding each other a tender adieu.

'I thank you, gentlemen,' said the Lieutenant, as we were getting into our chaise at the door of the inn. 'I thank you for your kind and faithful assistance in the most dreadful adventure of my life; if I should be so fortunate to get at the bottom of the mystery which hangs over that castle as I shall endeavour to do, I will take the first opportunity to appraise you of my success. Farewell, and do not forget your friend.'

At that the postillion smacked his whip and we went our different ways. On the fifth day we arrived, without any further incident, at the castle of Baron de R—, the father of my pupil. And here my narration ends.